The Crimson Raven: A Tale of Captain Poppie O'Malley

The Isles of Fate Series, Volume 1

Catherine J Rosser

Published by Catherine J Rosser, 2024.

This is a work of fiction. Similarities to real people, places, or events are entirely coincidental.

THE CRIMSON RAVEN: A TALE OF CAPTAIN POPPIE O'MALLEY

First edition. October 25, 2024.

ISBN: 979-8227611727

Written by Catherine J Rosser.

Table of Contents

To All the Pirate's at Heart

Chapter 1 – Fire in the Sky

The Irish coastline shimmered beneath the dying light of the setting sun, its rugged cliffs bathed in hues of gold and crimson. In the small fishing village of Ballyvaughan, the day was drawing to a close. The smell of salt and freshly caught herring lingered in the air as men returned from the sea, their boats creaking against the docks, and women gathered by the fire to prepare the evening meal.

Sixteen-year-old Poppie O'Malley stood on the edge of the shore, her feet buried in the cold, wet sand. Her wild red hair, inherited from her father, whipped around her face in the wind. She inhaled deeply, savoring the scent of the ocean—the only place she had ever truly felt free.

Behind her, the village buzzed with life, but Poppie's gaze remained fixed on the horizon. Every evening, she would stand there, looking out to sea, waiting for her father's return. Sean O'Malley was a fisherman, yes, but also something more. He was a man who sailed beyond the familiar waters, bringing back not just fish, but stories. Stories of distant lands, of pirates and treasure, and of a world much bigger than their little village.

"Poppie!" Her mother's voice called from the cottage behind her, breaking through her reverie. "Come help with supper. Your father'll be home soon."

Poppie sighed and turned, casting one last look at the horizon. There was a storm brewing in the distance, dark clouds gathering like a warning. She could feel it deep in her bones—a change was coming.

As she made her way back toward the cottage, she caught sight of a figure moving quickly along the path toward the docks. It was Old Finbar, the village elder, his weathered face creased with worry. He was muttering under his breath, something about strangers at the harbor.

Poppie felt a jolt of unease. Strangers were rare in Ballyvaughan. The village was too small, too isolated for many visitors. Her heart quickened as she watched Finbar disappear around the corner.

"What could he mean by strangers?" she wondered aloud. The thought nagged at her, but she shook it off. There were always tales of pirates lurking along the coast, but her father had never worried about them. "No pirate's daft enough to come this far north," he would say with a grin.

Yet, as she entered the cottage, the uneasy feeling clung to her like a shadow.

The meal was simple, as it always was. Bread, fish, and a stew made from what little vegetables they had left from the harvest. Her mother, Brigid, sat across from her, humming softly as she stirred the pot. Poppie's younger brother, Rory, tugged at her sleeve, his small face scrunched up with impatience.

"When's Da comin' back?" he asked for the hundredth time.

"Soon," Poppie said, though she was not so sure anymore.

The minutes ticked by, stretching into an hour, then two. Night had fallen, and the storm was now upon them. The winds howled outside, rattling the wooden shutters, and rain began to lash against the roof.

"He should've been home by now," Brigid said, her voice tight with worry.

Poppie exchanged a glance with her mother. It was not like her father to stay out this late, especially not with a storm like this. Something was wrong.

Without another word, Poppie grabbed her cloak and rushed to the door. "I'm going to the docks."

Brigid opened her mouth to protest but stopped herself. She knew better than anyone how stubborn Poppie could be when it came to her father. Instead, she simply nodded, her hands gripping the edge of the table.

Poppie stepped into the storm, pulling her cloak tight around her shoulders. The wind nearly knocked her off her feet as she made her way through the muddy streets toward the harbor. The village was dark, save for a few flickering lanterns swaying in the wind.

When she reached the docks, her heart sank.

There was no sign of her father's boat.

Instead, there were other ships—two of them—large, foreign vessels, their sails billowing in the gale. The crew aboard them moved like shadows, their faces obscured by the storm. Poppie's unease deepened. These were not merchants, and they were not from any nearby town.

As she watched, she saw Old Finbar again, this time arguing with one of the men from the ships. His voice, barely audible over the wind, sounded desperate. The man he spoke to was tall and broad-shouldered, with a thick beard and a sword hanging from his belt. A pirate.

Poppie's breath caught in her throat. Pirates. In her village.

Before she could move, before she could even think, a shout rang out from the harbor. Her father's voice.

"Get back, Brigid! Protect the children!" Poppie's father's desperate cry cut through the wind.

Poppie's heart leaped into her throat. She turned just in time to see him racing toward her, his face contorted with fear. But it was too late. Behind him, the pirates surged forward, cutting through the villagers like a pack of wolves. Swords gleamed in the lightning flashes, and the smell of smoke filled the air as one of the cottages went up in flames.

Poppie froze, her body paralyzed with terror. She had heard her father's stories of pirates, but nothing could have prepared her for the reality. The violence, the blood, the screams—it was too much.

"Poppie!" Her father's voice snapped her back to reality. "Run!"

But she did not run. Instead, she reached for the small knife she always kept hidden beneath her cloak. Her father had taught her how to wield it, though she had never imagined she would use it.

As one of the pirates charged toward her, she acted on instinct, thrusting the blade forward with all her strength. The man let out a grunt of pain as the knife found its mark, but he was much stronger than her. He yanked the blade from her grasp, his eyes dark with fury.

"Not bad for a lass," he sneered, raising his sword to strike.

Before the blow could fall, another figure appeared behind him—her father. With a savage roar, Sean O'Malley drove his own knife into the pirate's back, sending him crashing to the ground.

"Go, Poppie!" her father shouted. "Find your mother. Get to safety!"

Poppie hesitated, torn between running, and staying to fight. But she knew her father was right. She could not save him, not now. She had to protect her family.

With one last look at her father, Poppie turned and ran, her heart pounding in her chest. The village was in chaos—pirates everywhere, villagers fighting back with whatever they could find, flames licking at the thatched roofs of their homes.

She reached the cottage just in time to see her mother and Rory being dragged from the house by two pirates. Brigid struggled, trying to shield Rory with her body, but the pirates were relentless.

"Let them go!" Poppie screamed, throwing herself at the nearest pirate.

Her small fists were no match for the brute strength of the men, but she fought with everything she had. One of the pirates shoved her to the ground, laughing cruelly.

"This one's got spirit," he said, grabbing a fistful of her hair and yanking her to her feet.

Poppie cried out in pain, but she refused to show fear. She glared at the pirate, her green eyes blazing with defiance.

"Let her go," a voice growled from behind them.

The pirate stiffened, his grip on Poppie loosening. Slowly, he turned to face the newcomer. A tall man with a weathered face and a captain's coat stood before them, his hand resting on the hilt of his sword.

"Captain MacGregor," the pirate stammered. "We were just—"

"I said let her go," Captain Declan MacGregor repeated, his voice low and dangerous.

With a muttered curse, the pirate released Poppie, shoving her toward the ground. She stumbled but didn't fall, her eyes locked on the captain.

For a long moment, the two of them stared at each other—Poppie, bruised and defiant, and MacGregor, calm and unreadable.

Then, without a word, MacGregor turned and walked away, his men following behind him as the pirates withdrew from the village, leaving destruction in their wake.

Poppie watched them go, her body trembling with exhaustion. Her village was in ruins, her father lost to the sea, and her family torn apart.

But as she stood there, watching the pirate captain disappear into the storm, one thought burned in her mind.

This was not the end.

It was only the beginning.

Chapter 2 – The Storm Within

The storm raged on long after the pirates had gone. Rain fell in heavy sheets, dousing the flames that had consumed much of Ballyvaughan, but doing nothing to quell the destruction left in their wake. The once bustling village was now a ghost of itself. Smoke curled into the sky from charred rooftops, and the scent of salt mixed with the acrid stench of burnt wood and blood.

Poppie O'Malley stood among the wreckage, soaked to the bone, her body trembling from more than just the cold. Her hands shook as she clutched the small knife her father had given her, now slick with the blood of the pirate she had wounded. Her knuckles were white, her heart still hammering in her chest, refusing to believe what had just happened.

She turned her gaze toward the harbor, where the pirate ships had vanished into the storm, leaving nothing behind but broken homes and broken families. Her mother's sobs cut through the air behind her, but Poppie couldn't bring herself to turn around.

She couldn't face what she feared most.

Her father was gone.

"Poppie..." A soft, trembling voice reached her ears.

Slowly, she turned to see her mother, Brigid, kneeling in the mud, clutching Rory to her chest. Her face was streaked with tears, her body shaking as she tried to console the frightened boy. Rory's small frame shuddered with sobs, his face buried in their mother's shoulder.

Poppie swallowed hard, pushing back her own tears as she took a tentative step toward them. Every step felt like walking through water, her legs heavy with exhaustion and grief.

"Where's Da?" Rory's voice was small, barely a whisper, as he lifted his tear-streaked face toward Poppie.

Poppie froze, her throat tightening painfully. She couldn't bring herself to say the words. Not yet. Not now.

Instead, she dropped to her knees beside them, pulling both her mother and brother into her arms. They huddled together in the rain, the three of them, surrounded by the remnants of their world, broken and battered by the sea.

Hours passed, though it felt like days, as the storm finally began to relent. The rain turned to a light drizzle, and the winds softened, leaving behind only the low hum of waves crashing against the shore. The villagers had begun to emerge from their homes, faces drawn and weary as they surveyed the damage.

Poppie stood by the docks, her arms wrapped around herself, shivering in the cold. The rain had washed away the blood on her hands, but the stain of what had happened still clung to her like a second skin. She watched as Old Finbar and a few of the other fishermen scoured the shore for any sign of her father's boat.

"Sean was a good man," Finbar said quietly as he approached her. His eyes were bloodshot, his face lined with grief. "He fought hard to protect us."

Poppie's chest tightened, but she nodded, her lips pressed into a thin line.

"He's gone, isn't he?" Her voice was barely a whisper.

Finbar didn't answer immediately. He looked out at the sea, his face grim. "We've found no sign of him, lass. The pirates took many things from us tonight. Sean might be one of them."

Poppie clenched her fists, the familiar sting of tears threatening to spill over. But she refused to cry again. Not here. Not now. She had cried enough for one night.

Her father wasn't just a fisherman. He was a fighter, a protector. He would have given everything to keep the village safe. He *had* given everything.

"Those pirates," she began, her voice hardening as the weight of her grief turned into something colder, something sharper. "Do we know who they were?"

Finbar sighed, shaking his head. "Not entirely. But there were rumors of a crew led by a man named Bartholomew Graves—Black Bart, they call him. He's been terrorizing the coast for years, but we never thought he'd come this far north."

"Black Bart..." The name tasted bitter on her tongue.

It was more than just the loss of her father. It was the destruction of her home, the violation of everything they had worked for. And it was because of that man. Because of Black Bart and his crew of marauders.

"Where is he?" she asked, her voice steely with determination.

Finbar's brow furrowed as he studied her. "Lass, you don't want to be mixin' yourself up with the likes of him. Pirates like Bart don't just kill—they destroy everything in their path."

Poppie's eyes flashed with anger. "He's already destroyed everything."

The old man sighed heavily, his shoulders slumping. "Last I heard, Bart's been hiding out near the West Indies. The Caribbean is full of pirates like him, but it's a dangerous place, lass. Even for a man like your father, it'd be suicide to go after him."

Poppie swallowed, the weight of his words settling over her like a shroud. The Caribbean. It was a world away from everything she knew, a place where pirates ruled and laws were made at the edge of a blade.

But it didn't matter. The thought of staying in Ballyvaughan, living in the shadow of her father's death, was unbearable. She couldn't let Black Bart go unpunished. She couldn't just stand by and do nothing.

"I have to go," she said, more to herself than to Finbar.

The old man's eyes widened. "Go? To the Caribbean? Are you mad, girl? You wouldn't last a day out there!"

Poppie set her jaw, her heart pounding with determination. "I've lasted this long, haven't I? I'll find a way. I'll find him."

Finbar opened his mouth to argue, but the look in Poppie's eyes stopped him. He had seen that look before—the same look her father had whenever he set his mind on something. There would be no changing it.

With a heavy sigh, he nodded. "Then may God go with you, Poppie O'Malley. You'll need all the help you can get."

Later that night, Poppie sat by the fire in their now-quiet cottage. Her mother had finally fallen asleep, exhausted from the day's events, while Rory slept fitfully in the bed beside her. The storm outside had passed, but the storm within Poppie's heart raged on.

She stared into the flames, her mind racing with thoughts of revenge, of her father's face, of Black Bart's cruel laughter echoing through the village. The memories played over and over again in her mind, each one more painful than the last.

Her father had taught her many things—how to read the stars, how to navigate by the wind, how to fight when necessary—but he had never prepared her for this. He had never told her what to do when the world was ripped away from her.

The pirate captain who had spared her, Declan MacGregor, lingered in her thoughts as well. Why had he intervened? He could have let his men kill her, but he hadn't. Was it pity? Was it something more?

She clenched her fists, feeling the weight of her decision pressing down on her. If she wanted to survive—if she wanted to find Black Bart—she would need to learn more than just how to wield a knife. She would need to become something else. Something stronger.

A pirate.

The idea sent a chill through her. She had grown up hearing stories of pirates, of the brutality, the lawlessness. They were killers and thieves, but they were also free. Free to carve their own path in a world that had no place for them.

Poppie wasn't a child anymore. She couldn't wait for the world to make sense again. She had to take control. She had to find her own way.

Rising from her seat by the fire, she moved silently through the cottage, careful not to wake her mother or brother. She reached for the small satchel hanging by the door, filling it with what little food and supplies she could gather. Her fingers brushed over the leather-bound journal her father had kept—a book filled with maps, charts, and notes from his voyages.

She slipped it into her bag, her heart aching at the thought of leaving her family behind. But she couldn't stay. Not anymore. The path ahead was dangerous, but it was the only one that mattered.

As she stepped out into the cold night air, the stars glittered overhead, and the scent of the sea filled her lungs.

With one last glance at the village that had been her home, Poppie set her sights on the horizon.

She was going to find Black Bart.

And when she did, there would be no mercy.

Chapter 3 – The Rogue's Path

Poppie O'Malley slipped through the narrow alleys of Galway with her hood pulled low over her face. The bustling port town was a world away from the quiet village of Ballyvaughan. The streets were alive with merchants haggling over goods, sailors staggering out of taverns, and beggars lurking in every shadow. It smelled of fish, salt, and unwashed bodies—nothing like the clean sea air she had known back home.

Her heart raced as she moved through the crowd. She had been in Galway for a week now, searching for a ship that could take her far from the Irish coast. She knew her destination—the Caribbean—but getting there was another matter entirely. The journey would take months, and she had little money to her name.

She reached the docks and scanned the ships moored there, each one bearing a different flag from a different part of the world. Some were merchant vessels, loaded with cargo bound for Spain or France. Others, less reputable, bore the marks of privateers—legal pirates, commissioned by governments to attack enemy ships.

Poppie wasn't looking for a merchant or a privateer. She needed something more dangerous. She needed a pirate ship.

Her thoughts drifted to Captain Declan MacGregor, the pirate who had spared her life during the attack on Ballyvaughan. She didn't understand why he had done it, but something told her that crossing paths with him again might be the key to finding Black Bart.

But MacGregor was as elusive as the wind. No one in Galway had heard of him, and Poppie wasn't foolish enough to ask too many questions. Pirates were feared in these waters, and speaking their names too openly could lead to trouble.

As she wandered closer to the taverns, the rowdy laughter of sailors spilled out into the streets. This was where she needed to be—among men who lived their lives at sea, men who knew the world she was about to enter.

Her gaze fell on a small, dimly lit tavern tucked between two warehouses. The sign above the door swayed in the wind, its paint chipped and faded, but the name was still legible: **The Rogue's Path**.

Poppie took a deep breath and stepped inside.

The smell of stale beer and sweat hit her immediately. The room was packed with rough-looking men, some playing cards, others drinking heavily. A few of them cast curious glances her way, but most paid her no mind. She was just another traveler in a sea of strangers.

She made her way to the bar, where a grizzled old man with a scar running down his cheek was cleaning a mug with a rag that looked dirtier than the glass itself.

"Whatcha need, lass?" the bartender asked, eyeing her suspiciously.

Poppie lowered her hood just enough to meet his gaze. "I'm looking for passage," she said quietly, keeping her voice steady.

"Passage, eh? Where to?"

She hesitated for only a moment. "The Caribbean."

The bartender's hand paused mid-wipe, his eyes narrowing slightly. "That's a dangerous place, girl. You sure you know what you're gettin' into?"

"I know exactly what I'm getting into," she replied, her voice hardening.

He studied her for a long moment before nodding toward the back of the tavern. "Try the captain in the corner. He is headed that way, though he's not the type most folks want to sail with."

Poppie turned and spotted the man he was talking about. He sat alone at a small table, his boots propped up on the chair across from him. His long coat was worn, and his hat sat low on his brow, casting a shadow over his face. But even from across the room, Poppie could feel the air of danger that surrounded him.

She squared her shoulders and made her way over.

"Is this seat taken?" she asked, standing in front of him.

The man didn't move for a moment, then slowly lifted his head. His dark eyes gleamed with amusement as he looked her over. "Depends. You lookin' for a drink, or somethin' else?"

"Passage," she said. "To the Caribbean."

He raised an eyebrow, clearly surprised by her boldness. "And what would a little lass like you be wantin' in the Caribbean?"

Poppie met his gaze, her voice unwavering. "I have unfinished business there."

The captain leaned back in his chair, studying her with newfound interest. "Unfinished business? That sounds like trouble."

"I'm not afraid of trouble."

He chuckled, a low, dangerous sound. "No, I don't suppose you are." He tapped his fingers on the table, considering her offer. "Alright, girl. I'm headed for Tortuga. It's a rough place—cutthroats and thieves, the lot of them. But if you're set on goin', I won't stop you."

"Name your price," Poppie said, though she had little to offer.

The captain's eyes gleamed with mischief. "I don't need money, lass. What I need is a deckhand. Can you handle yourself aboard a ship?"

"I can learn."

"Good enough for me," he said with a grin. "I'm Captain Elias Drake, and I've got no room for the weak on my ship. If you can prove yourself useful, I'll take you as far as the Caribbean. If not... well, you'll find yourself swimming."

Poppie didn't flinch. "I'll take my chances."

Chapter 4 – Baptism by Storm

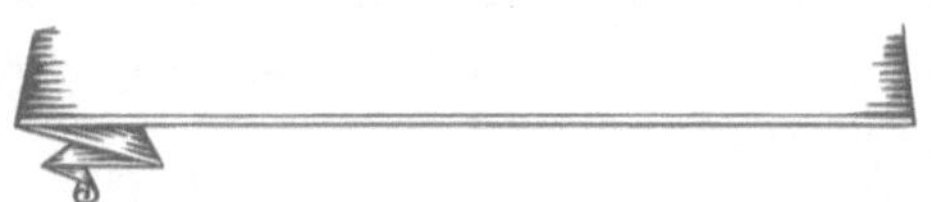

The **Seawraith** was a far cry from the fishing boats Poppie had known all her life. She had never been aboard a ship like this—sleek, fast, and dangerous, with sails the color of a stormy sky. The crew was as rough as Captain Drake had warned, a mix of men from every corner of the world, all of them hardened by life at sea.

Poppie had expected hostility, but for the most part, the crew left her alone. Perhaps they assumed she wouldn't last long, or maybe they had seen stranger things than a girl seeking passage to the Caribbean. Either way, they paid her little attention as she adjusted to life aboard the Seawraith.

The first days were grueling. Poppie had thought she was strong—she had grown up helping her father with the nets and boats—but this was something else entirely. Hauling ropes, scrubbing the decks, learning how to climb the rigging—it took every ounce of strength she had. Her hands were raw and blistered, her muscles ached, and the constant motion of the ship made her stomach churn.

But she didn't complain. She couldn't. There was too much at stake.

Every night, she lay in her cramped hammock, the sounds of the ocean lulling her into a restless sleep, her mind full of visions of Black Bart and the attack on Ballyvaughan. She held onto the anger, the grief, letting it fuel her through the exhaustion.

A week into their journey, a storm hit.

It started as a low rumble in the distance, barely more than a whisper on the wind. But within hours, the sky had darkened, the wind howling through the sails as waves crashed against the sides of the Seawraith.

"Everyone on deck!" Captain Drake's voice boomed over the chaos. "We're in for a rough one!"

Poppie scrambled out of her hammock, her heart pounding in her chest. She had been through storms before, but nothing like this. The ship lurched beneath her feet as she fought her way to the deck, where the crew was already hard at work securing the sails and battening down the hatches.

The wind lashed at her face, stinging her skin like needles. She grabbed hold of a rope and pulled with all her might, trying to steady the flailing sails. The rain came down in torrents, turning the deck into a slick, dangerous battlefield.

"Get up in the rigging!" someone shouted at her. "We need those sails tied down!"

Poppie didn't hesitate. She grabbed the nearest rope and started climbing, her fingers slipping on the wet lines. The wind howled in her ears, threatening to rip her from the rigging, but she forced herself to keep going.

Higher and higher she climbed until she reached the top of the mast, the ship swaying wildly beneath her. She tied off the sails with trembling hands, her heart racing as the storm raged around her.

Below her, Captain Drake bellowed orders, his voice barely audible over the roar of the storm. The crew moved like a well-oiled machine, their faces grim as they fought to keep the Seawraith from capsizing.

Suddenly, a massive wave crashed over the side of the ship, knocking several men off their feet. Poppie watched in horror as one of them was swept overboard, disappearing into the churning sea below.

For a brief moment, panic surged through her. This was madness. What was she doing here? She wasn't a sailor, she wasn't a pirate. She was just a girl from a small fishing village, chasing ghosts.

But then she remembered her father's face, the way he had fought to protect their home, and something inside her hardened. She wasn't just chasing ghosts. She was chasing justice.

With renewed determination, she gritted her teeth and secured the last of the sails, then began her descent. The storm was far from over, but Poppie O'Malley wasn't going to give up. Not now. Not ever.

As the storm continued to rage, she made her way back to the deck, soaked and exhausted but still standing.

And for the first time since leaving Ballyvaughan, she felt a spark of hope.

Chapter 5 – Shadows of Tortuga

The storm passed, but its memory lingered in the creaking timbers of the **Seawraith**. The crew, exhausted and battered, resumed their duties, but the fierce winds and crashing waves had shaken even the most hardened among them. For Poppie, it had been a baptism of fire—or rather, water. She had proven herself in the storm, and though the men still eyed her with suspicion, no one could deny her resolve.

Captain Drake hadn't spoken to her since the night of the storm, but Poppie knew he had been watching. His sharp eyes missed nothing. She wasn't just a deckhand anymore; she was something more, though she couldn't quite define what.

As the days stretched into weeks, the heat of the Caribbean sun replaced the cold winds of the Atlantic. The sea turned a deep, sapphire blue, and the air was thick with the smell of salt and sun-warmed wood. The promise of Tortuga lay ahead.

Poppie had heard the stories. Tortuga was a haven for pirates—a lawless port where the corrupt ruled and the brave died quickly. It was the kind of place where a girl like her could disappear... or find herself.

The **Seawraith** glided into Tortuga's harbor under the cover of dusk. The island rose before them like a dark, jagged shadow against the crimson sky. Fires burned along the docks, casting flickering light over the wooden shanties and taverns that clung to the shoreline like barnacles on a ship.

The port was alive with noise and movement—pirates, merchants, and sailors of every kind haggled over goods, brawled in the streets, and staggered out of taverns with drink in hand. It was a city of chaos and freedom, where the rules of the world no longer applied.

As the **Seawraith** docked, Poppie felt a knot tighten in her stomach. This was the edge of the world, a place where only the ruthless survived. But it was also the gateway to her revenge.

"You'll want to be careful here, lass," Captain Drake's voice came from behind her. She turned to find him standing at the ship's rail, his dark eyes scanning the harbor. "Tortuga's not for the faint of heart. The men here don't take kindly to strangers."

"I'm not afraid," Poppie said, though the truth was more complicated. Fear gnawed at the edges of her mind, but it was overshadowed by something stronger: the burning need to find Black Bart.

Drake gave her a knowing look. "I've no doubt. But there's a difference between being unafraid and being smart. Keep your head down, and you might just make it out of here alive."

Poppie nodded, though she had no intention of keeping her head down. She had come to Tortuga for one reason: to find information on Black Bart. And she wouldn't leave until she had it.

As the crew disembarked, Poppie followed them onto the docks. The smell of rotting fish, stale ale, and sweat assaulted her senses, but she pushed through the crowd, keeping her eyes sharp for any sign of trouble. She knew she stood out—a girl in a pirate's world—but she had learned quickly that the best way to survive was to act like you belonged.

She made her way toward one of the larger taverns near the dock, **The Broken Cutlass**. It was a sprawling, rickety building, its walls covered in graffiti and its windows broken or boarded up. Laughter, shouting, and the sound of shattering glass echoed from inside.

Taking a deep breath, Poppie pushed open the door and stepped into the chaos.

The tavern was packed with men—and a few women—drinking, gambling, and fighting. The air was thick with smoke and the stench of rum. No one paid her any mind as she slipped inside, which was exactly what she had hoped for.

She approached the bar, where a stout woman with graying hair and a scowl was serving drinks. Poppie pulled a coin from her pocket and slid it across the bar.

"Rum," she said.

The woman raised an eyebrow but said nothing as she poured the drink and set it down in front of her. Poppie took a sip, grimacing as the fiery liquid burned its way down her throat. She wasn't much for drinking, but she knew she couldn't look out of place.

She leaned in closer to the barmaid. "I'm looking for information," she said quietly.

The woman's scowl deepened. "Ain't we all, girl."

"This is different," Poppie pressed. "I'm looking for someone. Black Bart."

At the mention of the name, the barmaid froze, her eyes flicking up to meet Poppie's. For a moment, the noise of the tavern seemed to fade away, and Poppie could feel the weight of the woman's gaze.

"You don't want to be askin' about him," the barmaid said, her voice low and wary. "He's dangerous, even for a place like this."

"I know what he is," Poppie said, her voice hardening. "But I need to find him."

The woman hesitated, then leaned in closer, her voice barely more than a whisper. "Bart's been laying low. Word is he's planning something big, but no one knows where he is right now. If you're smart, you'll forget you ever heard his name."

Poppie's heart sank, but she refused to let it show. She wasn't leaving Tortuga empty-handed.

"Thank you," she said, sliding another coin across the bar before turning away.

As she moved through the tavern, her mind raced with thoughts of her next move. Bart was out there, somewhere, and if he was planning something big, she would find him.

She had to.

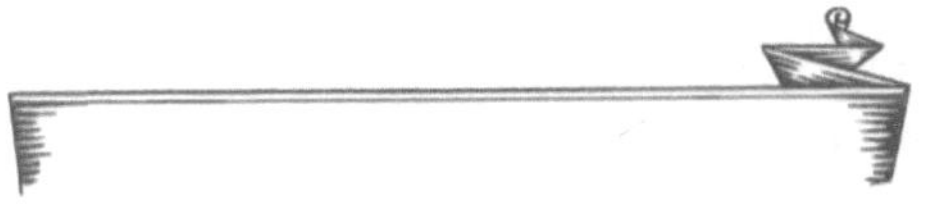

Chapter 6 – The Dagger's Edge

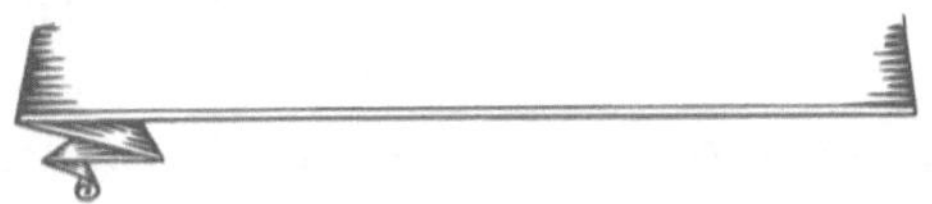

Poppie slipped through the crowded streets of Tortuga, her ears tuned to every whispered conversation and stray word. The barmaid's warning had only made her more determined. If Black Bart was in hiding, then she would dig deeper. She had nothing to lose.

As the night wore on, she made her way to a quieter part of the town, away from the noise and chaos of the main docks. The narrow alleyways here were lined with shadowy figures—smugglers, thieves, and worse. But Poppie was no stranger to danger.

She approached a small, run-down building with a faded sign that read **The Dagger's Edge**. This was where she'd been told she could find a man named Fergus MacCready, an information broker who supposedly knew everything that happened in Tortuga.

The door creaked open as she stepped inside. The dimly lit room was filled with the acrid scent of tobacco, and a few unsavory characters sat around small tables, whispering in hushed tones.

At the back of the room, behind a curtain of smoke, sat Fergus. He was a wiry man with a face like a weasel and eyes that darted nervously around the room as if he were always waiting for someone to stab him in the back.

Poppie approached him cautiously.

"Fergus MacCready?" she asked, keeping her voice low.

He looked up at her, his eyes narrowing in suspicion. "Who's askin'?"

"I need information," she said, sitting down across from him. "On Black Bart."

Fergus snorted, leaning back in his chair. "That's a name that'll get you killed, girl. Why would you be lookin' for a man like him?"

Poppie didn't flinch. "I have my reasons."

The weaselly man studied her for a long moment, then leaned forward, his voice dropping to a conspiratorial whisper. "Bart's a ghost. No one knows where he is, but word is he's gatherin' a fleet. Bigger than anythin' we've seen before. If he's comin' for you, you won't see him until it's too late."

Poppie's stomach clenched, but she forced herself to stay calm. "Where is he gathering this fleet?"

Fergus glanced around the room, then back at her. "There's a rumor that he's headed for Nassau. The governor there's been turnin' a blind eye to pirate activity. Could be he's plannin' to make his move from there."

"Nassau," Poppie repeated. It wasn't much, but it was a lead. And it was the first real piece of information she had gotten since arriving in Tortuga.

Fergus smirked. "But if you go after him, don't expect to come back. Bart's not the kind to leave loose ends."

"I don't intend to be a loose end," Poppie said, standing up and tossing a coin onto the table.

As she turned to leave, Fergus called after her. "You've got fire in you, girl. Don't let it burn you alive."

She didn't respond. She had what she needed.

Nassau.

Chapter 7 – Into the Lion's Den

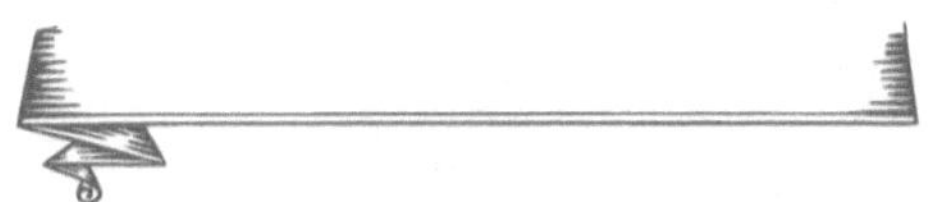

The **Seawraith** set sail from Tortuga under a brilliant blue sky. The sun beat down on the deck as the ship cut through the turquoise waters of the Caribbean, heading for Nassau. Captain Drake had raised an eyebrow when Poppie told him where she needed to go, but he didn't question her. He seemed to understand that she had her own path to follow.

The journey to Nassau was uneventful, but the tension that simmered beneath Poppie's skin was palpable. Every mile they sailed brought her closer to Black Bart, closer to the man who had torn her life apart.

As Nassau came into view, Poppie stood at the bow of the ship, her hands gripping the rail. The port was bustling with activity, larger and more organized than Tortuga. This was no pirate haven—it was a thriving colony, ruled by a governor who played both sides of the law.

The docks were crowded with merchant vessels, and the streets were filled with traders, soldiers, and sailors. But Poppie's eyes were fixed on the ships anchored in the harbor. Among them were several pirate vessels, their black flags hidden from view but unmistakable to those who knew what to look for.

Poppie felt a chill run down her spine. Somewhere in this city, Black Bart was waiting. And she was about to walk into the lion's den.

As the **Seawraith** docked, Poppie gathered her few belongings and prepared to disembark. Captain Drake approached her, his expression unreadable.

"You've got a dangerous road ahead of you," he said quietly. "Nassau's a different kind of beast."

"I know," Poppie replied.

Drake studied her for a moment, then nodded. "You've proven yourself, lass. But be careful. Bart's not like the others. He won't show mercy."

Poppie met his gaze. "Neither will I."

With that, she stepped off the ship and onto the bustling docks of Nassau. She had no plan, no allies, and no idea where to start. But she had her determination, and that was enough.

The hunt for Black Bart had truly begun.

Chapter 8 – The Governor's Web

Nassau was a world of contrasts. The port teemed with activity, the smell of exotic spices, tobacco, and sea salt thick in the air. Soldiers in crisp uniforms mingled with merchants in worn clothes, and though the law seemed to reign here, the undercurrent of pirate influence was undeniable.

Poppie felt the weight of every glance as she moved through the crowded streets. Nassau wasn't like Tortuga; it wasn't openly lawless, but the veneer of respectability was thin. The soldiers patrolling the streets might have worn the king's colors, but their pockets were lined with gold from the pirates they quietly tolerated.

Poppie had spent days quietly asking questions in the local taverns, probing for any mention of Black Bart. Rumors swirled that he was somewhere in the city, preparing for a major operation. But no one knew exactly where—or if they did, they were too afraid to say.

She had to be careful. Nassau was dangerous, not just because of Bart, but because of the governor who ruled the island, Governor Beaumont. He was a man of ambition, a manipulator who kept both pirates and the Crown in his pocket. Some said he was no better than a pirate himself.

One evening, Poppie found herself in a dimly lit tavern called **The Golden Fleece**, a favorite haunt of pirates who wanted to keep a low profile. She had learned by now that the best information often came from eavesdropping, so she sat quietly at a corner table, nursing a mug of ale and listening to the conversations around her.

A group of sailors nearby were whispering about a fleet being assembled in secret. Poppie's heart raced as she listened closer.

"Beaumont's turning a blind eye," one of them muttered. "Bart's payin' him well to keep the Redcoats off his back. They say it's goin' to be the biggest raid the Caribbean's ever seen."

Poppie's pulse quickened. This was the lead she had been waiting for.

Another sailor, a grizzled man with a long scar down his cheek, leaned in. "I heard the ships are anchored in a hidden cove west of the island. No one's seen 'em yet, but they'll be ready to sail soon. Word is, Bart's planning to strike at some Spanish treasure galleons headin' to Havana."

Poppie's mind raced. If Bart was building a fleet, it could mean the opportunity she had been waiting for. But she needed more than rumors—she needed to find Bart himself.

Later that night, as she slipped through the winding streets of Nassau, a voice called her name from the shadows.

"Poppie O'Malley."

Her hand instinctively went to the dagger at her waist as she turned. A man stepped out of the darkness, his face hidden beneath the brim of a wide hat. He moved with the confidence of someone who had seen too many battles to be afraid.

"Who are you?" she asked, her voice steady despite her racing heart.

"My name's Marcus Rooke," he said. "I hear you've been askin' about Black Bart."

Poppie's eyes narrowed. "What of it?"

Rooke smiled, his teeth flashing in the moonlight. "I know where to find him."

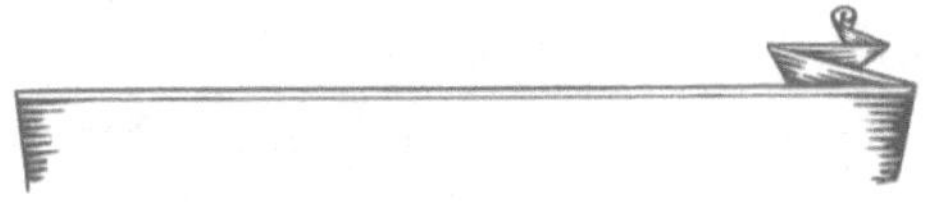

Chapter 9 – A Devil's Deal

Poppie's instincts screamed at her not to trust Marcus Rooke, but she was too close now to turn back. She followed him through the twisting alleys of Nassau until they reached a small, weathered building at the edge of the port. It was quiet, secluded, the kind of place where deals were made in the dark and lives were bought with silver.

Rooke led her inside and closed the door behind them, locking it with a flick of his wrist. The room was bare, save for a few crates and a rickety table. It smelled of old wood and damp sea air.

"Why are you helping me?" Poppie asked, her hand never leaving her dagger.

Rooke leaned against the wall, crossing his arms. "Let's just say Bart and I have unfinished business. I want him dead as much as you do."

Poppie raised an eyebrow. "And why should I believe you?"

He shrugged. "You don't have to. But I know you've been searchin' for him, and I have the information you need."

Poppie's grip tightened on her dagger. She hated being at someone else's mercy, especially someone as slippery as Rooke. But he had something she needed.

"Where is he?" she asked, cutting to the chase.

Rooke's smile widened. "Bart's keepin' himself hidden, but he's not far. He's holed up in a place called **Deadman's Cay**, an island off the coast. It's where he's been gatherin' his fleet."

Poppie's eyes widened. Deadman's Cay was infamous, a small, barren island that had served as a pirate hideout for years. It was the perfect place for Bart to build his operation in secret.

Rooke continued, his voice low. "He's got the governor's protection, but that won't last forever. If you want to catch him before he sails, you'll need to move fast."

Poppie's mind raced. Deadman's Cay was the break she had been waiting for, but it wouldn't be easy. Bart wouldn't be alone, and she couldn't take on an entire fleet by herself.

"What do you want in return?" she asked, her voice hard.

Rooke pushed himself off the wall and approached her, his eyes gleaming with something unreadable. "Just a share of the spoils when Bart's dead. And maybe... your loyalty."

Poppie's heart skipped a beat. Loyalty? To him? The idea was laughable, but she kept her face neutral.

"We'll see," she said, her voice cold.

Rooke chuckled, stepping back. "Fair enough. Get your crew ready. We leave at dawn."

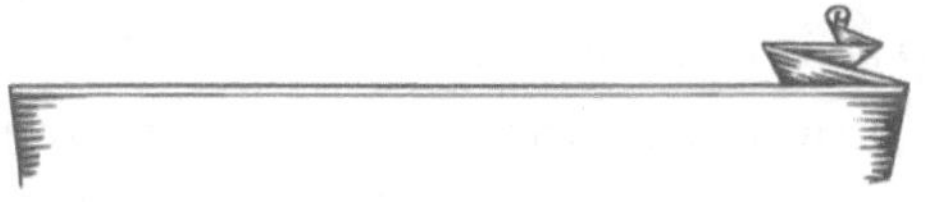

Chapter 10 – Deadman's Cay

The **Seawraith** sailed under a moonlit sky, the ocean calm and endless beneath them. Poppie stood at the bow, her eyes fixed on the horizon. The weight of the upcoming battle hung heavy on her shoulders. This was it. The moment she had been fighting for, the moment she would finally face Black Bart.

But doubt gnawed at her. Rooke's intentions were unclear, and she wasn't sure if she could trust him—or if she should trust anyone. Captain Drake had agreed to sail to Deadman's Cay, but even he had been wary of Rooke's involvement.

As the island came into view, a dark silhouette against the night sky, Poppie's pulse quickened. Deadman's Cay was desolate and foreboding, its jagged cliffs rising out of the sea like the teeth of some ancient monster. No lights, no signs of life—just darkness and the soft lapping of the waves against the shore.

Captain Drake approached her, his face grim. "We'll drop anchor here," he said. "I've seen enough pirate hideouts to know a trap when I see one."

Poppie nodded. "I'll take a small crew ashore. We need to be quiet. If Bart sees us coming, it's over."

Drake hesitated. "And Rooke?"

Poppie glanced over at the man, who stood at the stern of the ship, watching the island with a strange intensity.

"We keep an eye on him," she said.

Under the cover of darkness, Poppie and a handful of trusted crew members rowed a small boat toward the island. The air was thick with tension, every sound magnified by the silence of the night. As they approached the rocky shoreline, Poppie's heart raced. This was it.

They landed without incident, pulling the boat onto the beach and slipping into the shadows of the cliffs. Rooke led the way, his movements quick and sure. He seemed to know the island well, which only deepened Poppie's suspicion.

As they moved inland, the terrain grew rougher, the cliffs rising higher above them. The path twisted and turned, leading them deeper into the heart of the island.

Suddenly, Rooke stopped, holding up a hand for silence. Poppie tensed, her hand on the hilt of her sword.

"Up ahead," Rooke whispered. "Bart's camp is just beyond those cliffs."

Poppie's heart pounded in her chest. This was it. The moment she had been waiting for.

But as she moved to step forward, a sound behind her made her freeze. The click of a pistol being cocked.

"Don't move," a voice growled from the shadows.

Poppie's blood ran cold.

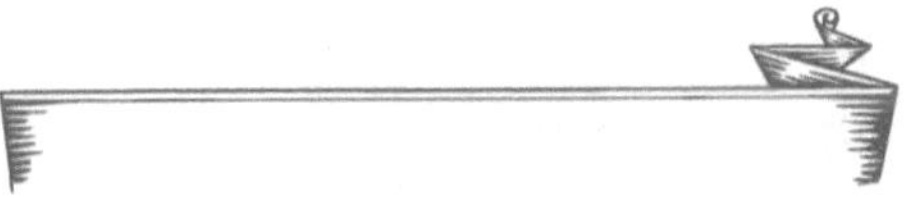

Chapter 11 – Betrayal in the Night

Poppie turned slowly, her heart hammering in her chest. Out of the shadows stepped a group of men, their faces hard and dangerous. They were pirates, armed with pistols and cutlasses, and their leader was a man Poppie recognized instantly.

Black Bart.

He was taller than she had imagined, with a weathered face and cold, calculating eyes. His long, black coat billowed in the breeze as he stepped forward, his pistol trained on her.

"Well, well," Bart said, his voice smooth and mocking. "What do we have here? A little bird who's flown too close to the flame."

Poppie's mind raced. How had they found her? Had Rooke betrayed her, led her straight into Bart's hands?

Bart's eyes flicked to Rooke, and the two men shared a look. Poppie's stomach dropped.

Of course. It had been a trap all along.

"I should've known," Poppie spat, her hand tightening on her sword. "You sold me out."

Rooke didn't deny it. He simply shrugged, a cold smile playing on his lips. "Business, Poppie. Nothing personal."

Bart chuckled. "Oh, it's personal for me, lass. You've been a thorn in my side for far too long."

Poppie's eyes blazed with fury. She had come so far, risked everything, only to be betrayed at the last moment. But she wasn't finished yet. She would fight, even if it was the last thing she did.

With a quick motion, she drew her sword, her heart pounding as the pirates around her moved in. The battle was about to begin.

Chapter 12 – Blood in the Moonlight

The sound of clashing steel rang out in the still night air. Poppie O'Malley's sword moved in swift arcs, parrying the onslaught of Black Bart's pirates. Her heart thundered in her chest as she fought for her life. Her mind buzzed with the betrayal she had just experienced. Marcus Rooke, the man who claimed to hate Bart as much as she did, had sold her out.

Rooke had melted into the shadows as soon as the fight began, leaving her to fend for herself. Poppie's crew, small but loyal, fought bravely by her side. Even Captain Drake had drawn his cutlass, though his face was grim—he had known from the start that Nassau's dealings would lead to danger.

Bart's men were well-trained, but they underestimated Poppie's ferocity. With a powerful strike, she disarmed one pirate and sent him sprawling. Another came at her with a pistol, but she ducked low, driving her blade into his leg. He fell with a scream.

"Poppie!" Drake shouted, cutting through a pirate who had lunged at him. "We can't win this fight. We need to retreat!"

Poppie's eyes flashed as she deflected another blow. Her fury was palpable, but she knew he was right. Bart's men outnumbered them. If they stayed, they'd be overwhelmed.

"We'll fall back to the cliffs!" she yelled, her voice carrying over the din of battle. "Regroup there!"

With that, she and her crew fought their way through the pirates, every step a struggle. Bart's mocking laughter echoed in her ears, but she didn't stop. Her anger fueled her, but her mind remained sharp. She couldn't die here—not before she had her vengeance.

As they neared the cliffs, Poppie caught sight of Rooke, watching from the shadows, his cold smile still in place. Their eyes met for a brief moment. The betrayal was clear. She knew now that he was playing both sides, a mercenary with no loyalty but to himself.

"Rooke!" Poppie snarled, but before she could reach him, he disappeared into the darkness once more.

The cliff edge loomed ahead, and Poppie and her crew scrambled up the rocky path, the sounds of pursuit close behind them. When they reached the top, they had only moments to catch their breath before Bart's men began their ascent.

"We hold them here!" Poppie ordered, her sword ready. "We hold the high ground!"

But even as the words left her mouth, she knew it was a losing battle. Bart's men were relentless, and they had nowhere to run. The cliff dropped steeply into the sea below, offering no escape.

Then, a shout came from behind them—Captain Drake, holding a length of rope.

"The sea, lass!" he shouted. "We'll jump!"

Poppie's heart pounded. It was madness, but it was their only chance. She sheathed her sword and grabbed the rope, her crew doing the same. One by one, they leapt from the cliff, the cold wind rushing past them as they plunged into the black water below.

The sea swallowed them whole, and the fight for survival continued.

Here are **Chapters 12 through 17** of *The Crimson Raven: A Tale of Poppie O'Malley*:

Chapter 12 – Blood in the Moonlight

The sound of clashing steel rang out in the still night air. Poppie O'Malley's sword moved in swift arcs, parrying the onslaught of Black Bart's pirates. Her heart thundered in her chest as she fought for her life. Her mind buzzed with the betrayal she had just experienced. Marcus Rooke, the man who claimed to hate Bart as much as she did, had sold her out.

Rooke had melted into the shadows as soon as the fight began, leaving her to fend for herself. Poppie's crew, small but loyal, fought bravely by her side. Even Captain Drake had drawn his cutlass, though his face was grim—he had known from the start that Nassau's dealings would lead to danger.

Bart's men were well-trained, but they underestimated Poppie's ferocity. With a powerful strike, she disarmed one pirate and sent him sprawling. Another came at her with a pistol, but she ducked low, driving her blade into his leg. He fell with a scream.

"Poppie!" Drake shouted, cutting through a pirate who had lunged at him. "We can't win this fight. We need to retreat!"

Poppie's eyes flashed as she deflected another blow. Her fury was palpable, but she knew he was right. Bart's men outnumbered them. If they stayed, they'd be overwhelmed.

"We'll fall back to the cliffs!" she yelled, her voice carrying over the din of battle. "Regroup there!"

With that, she and her crew fought their way through the pirates, every step a struggle. Bart's mocking laughter echoed in her ears, but she didn't stop. Her anger fueled her, but her mind remained sharp. She couldn't die here—not before she had her vengeance.

As they neared the cliffs, Poppie caught sight of Rooke, watching from the shadows, his cold smile still in place. Their eyes met for a brief moment. The betrayal was clear. She knew now that he was playing both sides, a mercenary with no loyalty but to himself.

"Rooke!" Poppie snarled, but before she could reach him, he disappeared into the darkness once more.

The cliff edge loomed ahead, and Poppie and her crew scrambled up the rocky path, the sounds of pursuit close behind them. When they reached the top, they had only moments to catch their breath before Bart's men began their ascent.

"We hold them here!" Poppie ordered, her sword ready. "We hold the high ground!"

But even as the words left her mouth, she knew it was a losing battle. Bart's men were relentless, and they had nowhere to run. The cliff dropped steeply into the sea below, offering no escape.

Then, a shout came from behind them—Captain Drake, holding a length of rope.

"The sea, lass!" he shouted. "We'll jump!"

Poppie's heart pounded. It was madness, but it was their only chance. She sheathed her sword and grabbed the rope, her crew doing the same. One by one, they leapt from the cliff, the cold wind rushing past them as they plunged into the black water below.

The sea swallowed them whole, and the fight for survival continued.

Chapter 13 – The Depths of Despair

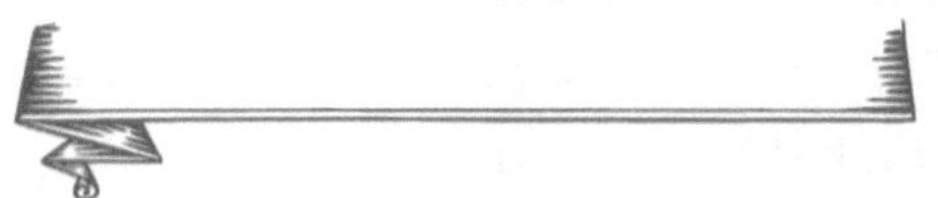

The ocean was frigid, the waves crashing against the jagged rocks of Deadman's Cay. Poppie struggled to keep her head above water, her body exhausted from the fight. The cold bit into her skin, but she forced herself to swim, her muscles burning with the effort.

Captain Drake surfaced beside her, gasping for breath. "We need to get to the cove!" he shouted over the roar of the sea.

Poppie nodded, though she could barely hear him. She could see the cove in the distance, a small inlet where they had left their rowboat. If they could reach it, they might have a chance to escape.

But the swim was grueling, the waves battering them with every stroke. Her crew fought valiantly, but the sea was merciless. Two of her men were swept away by the current before they could even reach the shore.

Poppie gritted her teeth and pushed herself harder. She couldn't let them die in vain. Not after everything they had been through. She had come too far to lose now.

After what felt like an eternity, they reached the cove. Poppie dragged herself onto the rocky shore, her body trembling with exhaustion. Drake was beside her, panting heavily, his face pale in the moonlight.

"We... made it," he gasped, collapsing onto the rocks.

Poppie's chest heaved as she looked back toward the sea. In the distance, she could still see the flicker of torches on the cliffs. Bart's men would soon discover their escape, but for now, they had bought themselves some time.

"Rooke," Poppie muttered under her breath, her eyes narrowing. "I'll kill him for this."

Drake sat up, shaking his head. "He'll pay, lass. But right now, we need to focus on gettin' off this cursed island."

Poppie nodded, though her mind was consumed with thoughts of revenge. She had been so close to Bart, and Rooke had taken that from her. But she couldn't dwell on it now. They needed to survive first.

They gathered what remained of their crew and set to work on the rowboat. It was their only way off the island, and it would have to be enough. As they prepared to set sail, Poppie couldn't shake the feeling that this was only the beginning of something much darker.

Chapter 14 – The Return to Tortuga

The journey back to Tortuga was somber. Poppie's crew was smaller now, their numbers thinned by both Bart's men and the merciless sea. The survivors were exhausted, their spirits dampened by the failure at Deadman's Cay.

Poppie stood at the helm of the **Seawraith**, her face set in a mask of determination. She had lost this battle, but the war was far from over. Black Bart had slipped through her fingers, but she wouldn't rest until she found him again.

Captain Drake approached her, his expression grave. "We'll need to regroup, lass," he said quietly. "Bart's fleet is still out there, and he won't stop 'til he's got what he wants."

Poppie nodded, though her mind was elsewhere. Tortuga would be a temporary refuge, a place to lick their wounds and plan their next move. But she knew that Nassau and Deadman's Cay were still under Bart's influence, and she couldn't risk another direct attack.

"I need information," Poppie muttered, more to herself than to Drake.

"Aye," Drake agreed. "But where do we start? Rooke's gone, and Bart's not easy to track."

Poppie's jaw tightened. "We start by finding Rooke. He knows more than he's letting on."

Drake sighed, his weathered face creased with worry. "Aye, but that man's slippery as an eel. He'll be long gone by now."

Poppie's eyes hardened. "Then I'll hunt him to the ends of the earth if I have to."

Tortuga appeared on the horizon, its chaotic sprawl a familiar sight. Poppie's heart stirred with the knowledge that this island held the answers she needed. Somewhere in this lawless place, she would find Rooke. And when she did, she would make him pay for his betrayal.

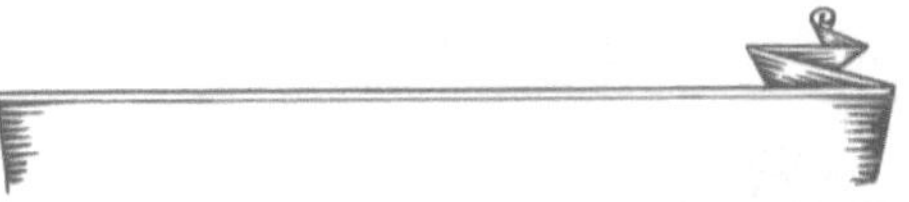

Chapter 15 – The Price of Vengeance

Tortuga had always felt like a den of vipers, but now, to Poppie, it was personal. Every shadow seemed to hold a threat, every whisper a potential lead on Rooke. She had been betrayed once; she wouldn't let it happen again.

The first few days were fruitless. Poppie scoured the taverns, the back alleys, the docks—anywhere Rooke might hide. But he was a ghost, slipping away just as she thought she was closing in. Still, Poppie was relentless. She knew he was here somewhere. Tortuga was too small for a man like Rooke to disappear completely.

One night, after hours of searching, she found herself back at **The Silver Serpent**, the tavern where she had first met Captain Drake. The place was crowded as always, filled with pirates and mercenaries drinking away their spoils. Poppie sat at a table in the corner, her eyes scanning the room for any sign of her quarry.

As she nursed her drink, a familiar face appeared at the door. A tall, lean man with a wicked scar down his cheek—Marcus Rooke.

Poppie's heart skipped a beat. She had found him at last.

Without hesitation, she rose from her seat and made her way through the crowd, her hand resting on the hilt of her sword. Rooke didn't notice her until it was too late. Poppie grabbed him by the collar and shoved him into a nearby alley, pinning him against the wall.

"Hello, Rooke," she hissed, her eyes burning with fury.

Rooke's grin faltered, but only for a moment. "Well, well. The little raven's still alive."

Poppie pressed the tip of her dagger against his throat. "You betrayed me."

Rook's cocky grin faltered, but only for a moment. "Business, Poppie. Nothing personal."

She pushed the dagger harder, just enough for him to feel the cold steel against his skin. "You cost me my chance at Bart."

Rooke's eyes flicked to the side, scanning the alley. Poppie knew he was calculating his next move, but she had the upper hand this time. Her grip tightened on his collar, and he winced.

"Easy, girl," he said, raising his hands. "I didn't have much of a choice. Bart doesn't take kindly to being double-crossed, and I've got a survival instinct, if you haven't noticed."

Poppie's heart pounded in her chest. "You're going to help me find him," she said, her voice low and threatening. "Or I'll make sure you don't survive this."

Rooke's grin returned, though it was weaker now. "You've got spirit, I'll give you that. But you're not thinking clearly. Bart's fleet is nearly complete. He's got half the Caribbean in his pocket, and once he sails, no one—*no one*—will be able to stop him."

Poppie leaned in closer, her face inches from his. "I don't care about his fleet. I want Bart. Dead."

Rooke sighed, his shoulders slumping. "All right, all right. I can get you close to him, but you're walking into a death trap.

You need more than just a knife and a grudge to take down Black Bart."

She narrowed her eyes. "Tell me where he is."

Rooke hesitated for a long moment, weighing his options. Finally, he sighed again. "There's a place, just off the northern coast of Hispaniola. Bart's been using it as a base of operations. It's a fortress, Poppie—well-guarded, well-stocked. You'll need more than just your crew to storm it."

Poppie pulled back, her dagger still at the ready. "Let me worry about that. You'll take me there."

Rooke raised an eyebrow. "Oh, I will, will I?"

She leaned in, her voice a dangerous whisper. "If you want to live."

The smirk faded from his face. He knew she was serious. With a reluctant nod, he agreed. "Fine. But once we get there, you're on your own."

Poppie lowered the dagger, stepping back to give him room to breathe. "Good. Now get moving. We leave at dawn."

Chapter 16 – The Fortress of Hispaniola

The journey to Bart's fortress was tense and silent. Rooke, true to his word, led Poppie and her crew through the treacherous waters off the northern coast of Hispaniola. The sea was calm, but the tension aboard the **Seawraith** was palpable.

Poppie stood at the bow, staring at the horizon. The fortress loomed ahead—a dark shape rising from the cliffs, surrounded by treacherous reefs and jagged rocks. It was an imposing sight, but Poppie felt no fear. Only the burning desire for vengeance.

"Bart's got men patrolling the waters," Rooke said, standing beside her. "We'll need to slip in under cover of darkness."

Poppie nodded. "We'll land on the western shore, near the cliffs. From there, we can make our way up to the fortress."

Drake approached; his face grim. "This isn't going to be easy, lass. Bart's men are everywhere."

"I know," Poppie replied. "But this is our only chance."

Drake studied her for a moment, then nodded. "We'll be ready."

As night fell, the **Seawraith** slipped into the shadows of the cliffs. The crew rowed silently toward the shore, their oars barely making a sound in the still water. Poppie's heart raced as they neared the rocky beach. The fortress loomed above them, a dark silhouette against the night sky.

Once ashore, Poppie led her crew up the steep cliffs, their movements quiet and deliberate. The path was narrow and treacherous, but they pressed on, the weight of their mission driving them forward.

As they reached the top, the fortress came into full view. It was massive, with towering walls and heavily armed guards patrolling the perimeter. Poppie crouched behind a boulder, her eyes scanning the defenses.

"We'll need to create a distraction," Drake whispered. "Something to draw the guards away from the main gate."

Poppie nodded. "Rooke, you're up."

Rooke, who had been silently watching the fortress, glanced at her. "And what exactly do you want me to do?"

"Get inside," Poppie said. "You're the one who knows this place. You'll find a way to get the guards' attention."

Rooke hesitated, then gave a resigned nod. "Fine. But don't expect me to come back for you."

"I won't," Poppie said, her voice cold.

Rooke disappeared into the shadows, and Poppie turned to Drake. "Once the guards are distracted, we move in. We'll go through the southern gate—it's less guarded."

Drake nodded. "And then?"

"Then we find Bart," Poppie said, her eyes hard. "And we finish this."

Moments later, the sound of shouting echoed from the fortress. Rooke had done his job. The guards rushed toward the commotion, leaving the southern gate unguarded.

Poppie signaled to her crew, and they moved swiftly and silently toward the gate. The tension was thick as they slipped inside, their footsteps barely audible on the stone floor.

The fortress was a labyrinth of dark corridors and hidden chambers, but Poppie moved with purpose. She knew Bart would be in the heart of the fortress, surrounded by his most loyal men. Her sword was ready, her heart pounding with anticipation.

They rounded a corner, and there he was.

Black Bart.

He stood at the far end of the room, his back to them, surrounded by a handful of his men. The moment he turned and saw her, his face twisted into a cold smile.

"Well, well," Bart said, his voice dripping with mockery. "The little raven has returned."

Poppie's hand tightened on her sword. "This ends now."

Chapter 17 – The Final Reckoning

The room fell silent, the tension thick as Poppie faced down the man who had destroyed her life. Black Bart's cold, calculating eyes gleamed in the dim light, his smirk growing as he surveyed the small group of rebels standing before him.

"Do you really think you can take me, girl?" Bart's voice was low, dangerous. "I've seen hundreds like you. Filled with vengeance, fueled by rage. And every single one of them fell by my hand."

Poppie's blood boiled. Her grip on the hilt of her sword tightened, and she took a step forward. "I'm not like the others."

With a flick of his wrist, Bart signaled to his men, and they drew their weapons, circling Poppie and her crew. The odds were stacked against them, but Poppie's resolve was unshakable.

"I've been waiting for this moment," Poppie said, her voice steady, though her heart raced with adrenaline. "You killed my father. You destroyed my home. And now, I'll destroy you."

Bart chuckled, shaking his head. "You're a fool, girl. You should've stayed in the shadows where you belong."

Poppie lunged forward, her sword flashing in the dim light. Bart's men moved to intercept her, but she cut through them with fierce precision, her anger fueling every strike. Behind her,

Drake and the rest of her crew fought valiantly, holding their own against the wave of pirates.

Bart watched with a cold, detached gaze, his sword still sheathed. He waited, watching Poppie carve her way through his men, as if testing her strength. And then, when the last of his men fell, he drew his sword.

Poppie's chest heaved with exertion as she faced Bart, her sword poised for the final battle.

"Now," Bart said, his voice low and menacing. "Let's see what you're really made of."

He moved with the speed and precision of a seasoned fighter, his blade flashing as he struck at Poppie. She barely had time to parry the blow, the force of his attack nearly knocking her off balance. He was stronger than she had expected, and his experience showed in every calculated move.

But Poppie was no longer the girl from Ballyvaughan. She had survived battles, storms, and betrayals. She had fought her way across the Caribbean, driven by the need for vengeance. And now, that fire burned brighter than ever.

Their swords clashed in a deadly dance, each strike more brutal than the last. Poppie's breath came in ragged gasps, but she refused to give in. She would not let Bart win.

Bart's blade cut through the air, a deadly arc aimed at Poppie's throat. She twisted just in time, the sharp edge grazing her neck but leaving her unscathed. Pain radiated from the wound on her shoulder, but she ignored it, focusing all her energy on the man in front of her. Black Bart fought like a demon, his strikes relentless, each one aimed to kill. But Poppie wasn't about to let him win. Not after everything he had taken from her.

She met each of his attacks with swift, precise parries, her eyes burning with determination. Memories of her father, her village, her lost home flashed before her. The rage simmered, but beneath it was something stronger: resolve. She wasn't just fighting for revenge anymore. She was fighting for herself, for her future.

"You should have stayed out of this, girl," Bart sneered, circling her like a predator. "Your father was a fool, and now you'll die just like him."

Poppie's eyes blazed. "You took everything from me," she spat. "I'll never stop until you're dead."

Bart laughed, a deep, sinister sound. "Then let's finish this."

He lunged at her, faster than before, his blade aiming for her heart. Poppie sidestepped, deflecting his strike with a sharp clang. Her muscles burned with exhaustion, but she pressed on, driving Bart back with a series of quick, brutal blows. Bart stumbled, surprise flickering across his face. For the first time, he realized she wasn't the same girl he had terrorized all those years ago.

Summoning her last reserves of strength, Poppie went on the offensive. She feinted left, then slashed right, catching Bart off guard. Her blade cut across his chest, drawing a deep, bloody line. Bart growled in pain, clutching his wound.

"You've fought well," Bart hissed, blood dripping from his mouth. "But you'll never be strong enough to kill me."

Poppie stepped forward, her sword raised. Her voice was ice. "Watch me."

With a final surge of energy, she brought her blade down with all her might. Bart tried to parry, but he was too slow, too wounded. Her sword sliced through his defenses, burying itself deep into his chest. Bart gasped, his eyes wide with shock as he staggered backward.

For a moment, the room was silent. Bart's sword clattered to the ground, and his knees buckled as he fell. His hand reached for the wound in his chest, blood pooling around him. Poppie stood over him, her breath ragged, her heart pounding in her ears.

Bart's eyes met hers, the life slowly draining from them. "You... won't... stop me," he rasped.

Poppie knelt beside him, her voice steady. "I already have."

With one final breath, Black Bart, the pirate who had terrorized the Caribbean, slumped forward and was still.

Poppie stood, her sword dripping with his blood. The weight of the moment pressed down on her, but she felt no relief, no joy. Only a deep, hollow sense of finality. She had done it. The man who had taken her father, her home, and nearly her life, was dead.

Captain Drake and the rest of her crew, bloodied but alive, gathered around her. The battle was over. They had won.

Drake approached, wiping his bloodied sword on his coat. "It's done, lass. Bart's gone."

Poppie nodded, her eyes never leaving Bart's lifeless body. "It's over."

But even as the words left her lips, she knew that nothing would ever be the same. Revenge had consumed her for so long, driven her to this moment. Now, standing in the aftermath of her victory, she realized there was more to life than vengeance.

She sheathed her sword and turned to face her crew. "Let's get off this cursed island."

Epilogue – The Crimson Raven

The **Seawraith** sailed smoothly through the turquoise waters of the Caribbean, its sails billowing in the warm breeze. The sky was clear, the sun bright above, and the crew worked diligently, their spirits lifted by their recent victory. Black Bart's fleet had crumbled after his death, and the seas were, for now, a little safer.

Poppie stood at the helm, the wind tugging at her hair, her eyes scanning the horizon. She had changed so much since the day she left Ballyvaughan. The girl she had been was gone, replaced by a hardened, battle-scarred woman who had carved her name into the very seas she sailed.

But despite everything she had lost, Poppie had found something unexpected: freedom. She was no longer bound by the chains of vengeance. She had earned the respect of her crew, forged new alliances, and built a future for herself beyond the shadows of her past.

As the ship sailed toward the horizon, Captain Drake approached her, a rare smile on his weathered face. "Where to next, Captain O'Malley?"

Poppie glanced at him, her eyes gleaming with newfound purpose. "Anywhere the wind takes us."

Drake chuckled. "Aye, the world's ours now."

Poppie nodded, feeling the weight of her future on her shoulders. She had a ship, a crew, and a name that would be feared across the seas: The Crimson Raven. But most importantly, she had her freedom.

As the **Seawraith** sailed into the endless blue, Poppie O'Malley smiled, ready for whatever adventures lay ahead. The seas were hers now, and nothing could stop her.

Don't miss out!

Visit the website below and you can sign up to receive emails whenever Catherine J Rosser publishes a new book. There's no charge and no obligation.

https://books2read.com/r/B-A-FGQOC-XYRDF

BOOKS 2 READ

Connecting independent readers to independent writers.

But Aelia's magic isn't just a gift—it's a responsibility. Tied to the flow of time itself, her power allows her to age slowly, keeping her unchanged while the world around her moves forward. As she struggles to accept this truth, a darker force emerges: the Shadowborne, a secretive and ruthless group hunting those with magic like hers. They will stop at nothing to control or destroy the ancient power she now wields.

Guided by a deep connection to the magic within her and a newfound ally, Kaelen, Aelia must navigate a world where magic is both revered and feared. Along the way, she learns that her family has been hidden and protected, but at a cost—memories of her are slowly fading from their minds. Saddened but resolute, Aelia leaves them in peace, knowing that their safety comes first.

Now, with the Shadowborne closing in and her family protected, Aelia must embrace her power, learn to master the magic she once feared, and prepare for the battle ahead. Her journey has only just begun.

The Magic Within is the first thrilling installment of **The Eternal Magic Series**, an epic tale of magic, immortality, and destiny. Aelia's path will lead her through centuries, but first, she must confront the power within and the enemies who seek to control it.

Read more at https://catherinejrosser.com/.

Also by Catherine J Rosser

The Eternal Magic Series
The Magic Within

The Isles of Fate Series
The Crimson Raven: A Tale of Captain Poppie O'Malley

Standalone
Beyond the Horizon
Echoes in the Abyss
Haven Falls
The Fractured Mind
The Next Chapter: Embracing Midlife with Purpose, Peace, and
Possibility
The Thistle Queen

Watch for more at https://catherinejrosser.com/.

About the Author

Catherine J. Rosser is a fantasy author who weaves together myth, magic, and unforgettable journeys. Known for her vivid storytelling and rich characters, she brings epic worlds to life with themes of destiny and self-discovery. When not writing, Catherine draws inspiration from nature, channeling its beauty into her imaginative tales.

Read more at https://catherinejrosser.com/.

www.ingramcontent.com/pod-product-compliance
Lightning Source LLC
Chambersburg PA
CBHW031459130726
47989CB00003B/1463